# Nobody Wants Barkley

## Marilyn D. Anderson

### illustrated by Mel Crawford

*For my nieces—*
*Katie, Brenda, Meagan, and Joni*

## ◢▮PAGES™

Fifth printing by Willowisp Press 1997.

Published by Willowisp Press
801 94th Avenue North, St. Petersburg, Florida 33702

Printed in the United States of America

6 8 10 9 7 5

ISBN 0-87406-808-8

# One

"Ruff, ruff!" Barkley announced. He saw black and white monsters in the field next door. He wanted his master, Jamie Boggs, to do something about it. He looked pleadingly up at Jamie, who was busy tying his shoes. "Ruff, ruff," Barkley repeated.

"No, Barkley," Jamie said firmly, using one of the few commands Barkley knew. "Those are just cows, and they're supposed to be in that field."

The whiskery-faced dog stopped barking. He crouched down and wiggled his way toward Jamie. Leaning against Jamie's chest, he licked the boy's face to show he was sorry for making

3

such a fuss. But how was a city dog supposed to know about cows? Barkley wondered.

It had been two months now since Barkley's family moved all the way from beautiful Elm Street in New York to Indiana. But Barkley felt as if it had been years.

Jamie and his parents had driven out to Indiana in early June, and Barkley was supposed to fly out on a plane to join them. But the dog had gotten out of his carrier at the airport and spent weeks being lost. He'd walked down many hot, dusty roads and through lots of corn fields trying to find the Boggs family.

Now that Barkley and his family were back together, everything should have been perfect. But it wasn't.

Indiana was boiling hot in the summertime. And the new place wasn't fun like Elm Street had been. Barkley and Jamie used to do lots of neat things with Jamie's friends in New York. Here Jamie never seemed to do anything exciting.

When he first arrived, Barkley had tried to liven things up. He knocked over all the wastebaskets in the house and went from room to room decorating with toilet tissue.

But no one had thought it was funny. Instead, the family got mad and scolded him. Barkley didn't know what they said, but he knew it wasn't good. So now, the dog just moped around and waited for Jamie to play with him.

This morning, Barkley had gone downstairs for breakfast as usual. He had found Jamie and his mom talking in the kitchen.

"Jamie," said Mrs. Boggs, "it's such a nice day. Why don't you go outside and play?"

"By myself?" Jamie protested.

"No," she said. "Take Barkley."

Barkley's ears perked up at the sound of his name.

"All right," Jamie said.

So now Barkley and Jamie were out in the yard looking for something to do. Barkley was hoping Jamie would act like he used to and be happy.

But as soon as he finished tying his shoes, Jamie wandered around the yard aimlessly. Barkley trailed sadly behind him. He thought about barking to get his boy's attention. But he decided he might get into trouble again, and he hated to get yelled at.

Then Jamie stopped. He looked off into the woods behind the house. Barkley craned his neck to see what was so important. All he could see was trees.

"Did you hear that noise?" Jamie asked. "It sounded like some kind of an animal."

Barkley had heard a noise. But after getting in trouble for barking at the cows, he hadn't dared make another sound. Now he looked up at Jamie and wagged his tail.

Jamie started walking toward the trees. His steps quickened. Barkley began to trot in circles around the boy, hoping they'd have a race or play a game. But Jamie just kept walking. He didn't even glance at Barkley.

They came to a barbed wire fence, and Jamie rolled underneath it. Barkley quickly ducked his head to follow. He was feeling excited. He sensed that maybe he and Jamie were on an adventure at last.

The scattered trees and blackberry thickets that dotted the hills beyond the fence were home to all kind of animals. Barkley set out to investigate each of their fascinating smells.

Jamie seemed happier now too. He started to whistle, and he picked up a stick to swing as they walked along.

After a while, Barkley saw a small pond in the distance. He trotted toward it, hoping to take a swim. Then something else caught his attention. A group of woolly animals were grazing nearby. They looked so soft and gentle that Barkley bounded toward them.

But just as Barkley reached the nearest creature, it stamped its foot at him. The dog jumped back in surprise.

"Ruff?" he said softly. He was confused. The animal had seemed friendly, but it certainly wasn't.

Barkley waited to see what would happen next. The animal nearest him bolted back to where its friends waited. Barkley looked back at Jamie for some hint of what to do.

Then he heard the sound of running feet. The whole flock of fuzzy animals was racing away. Barkley was delighted. He figured they wanted to play tag. Barkley liked tag, so he charged after them.

"Barkley, come back!" Jamie shouted. But the dog was having too much fun to listen. He galloped on after the woolly animals. He wondered why Jamie didn't want to play tag too.

The animals ran and ran. Barkley stayed close on their heels, and at last Jamie was running along behind. The animals ran until they came to some farm buildings.

Suddenly a huge German shepherd appeared and Barkley froze in his tracks. The

other dog looked startled at the sight of Barkley, and it stood at attention for a moment. Then a big man with dark bushy hair and a boy about Jamie's size walked up behind the huge dog.

"What's going on here?" the man demanded. "How come this dumb mutt is chasing my sheep?"

Barkley cringed. It sounded like he was in trouble again. He ran over to Jamie for help, but he sensed Jamie was scared too.

"I'm sorry, mister," Jamie said, panting. "Barkley just wanted to play."

"Is that so?" the man growled. "Let me give you some advice. Dogs who run loose and chase livestock sometimes get hurt. Do you know what I mean?"

"Yes, sir," Jamie said quickly. "I understand. We just moved here, and I didn't know about your sheep."

The man's eyes narrowed. "From the city, I'll bet," he sneered. "Well, I don't want to see that dog on my property again. Or else!"

Barkley watched as Jamie and the man talked. He knew he and Jamie were both in trouble. He wished he could help. Finally the humans stopped talking and Jamie looked down at him.

Jamie gave Barkley a nod, and they hurried away from the nasty man. Soon they began to run. They ran until they were safely back inside their house. Jamie collapsed on the couch, and Barkley dropped to the floor nearby to pant.

Mrs. Boggs ambled into the living room and said, "You're home already?"

"Yeah," said Jamie.

"Hmm," she said, frowning. "Well, okay. I want you to go up and take a shower. We need to go into town and buy you some school clothes this afternoon."

"Can Barkley go along?" Jamie asked.

Barkley heard his name and looked up. He wagged his tail hopefully.

Jamie's mom looked down at the dog and smiled. "I guess so," she said.

# Two

Barkley scrambled into the front seat of the car to sit next to Jamie. He was excited to be going for a ride. To say thanks, he bounced around and tickled Jamie's ears with his tongue. Then he headed over to Mrs. Boggs. He wanted to be nice to her too.

"Barkley!" she squealed. "I have to drive. Jamie, please put him in the back seat."

"Okay," the boy agreed.

He dumped Barkley onto the floor behind him. Barkley felt sad for a moment. But then he realized that he could look out both windows this way. He ran back and forth to press his nose against first the right window and then the left.

Mrs. Boggs started the car and they began to move. All Barkley could see at first was a corn field on one side and a bunch of trees on the other. Then they passed a house with some kids playing in a sandbox out front. Barkley pressed his nose against the window harder and wagged his tail. He loved kids more than just about anything.

Next Barkley saw a house that seemed to be falling apart. It needed paint, and the grass around it was too tall. But the lady who rocked on the front porch swing didn't seem to mind.

"What a junky place," Jamie observed.

"Yes, I'm afraid poor old Mrs. Williams has a hard time of it," said his mother. "I've heard a lot about her."

Barkley couldn't understand what they were mumbling about, but by now they were going by a third house. This one was made of brick and had a garage attached. Two boys about Jamie's size were shooting baskets in the driveway. Barkley wagged his tail again. Those boys were having fun.

"Look, Jamie," said Mrs. Boggs. She pointed out the window. "There *are* other boys in this neighborhood. Maybe you could meet them and play basketball together. Or you could invite them over to our house."

Jamie made a face and shook his head. He looked sadly out the window, but said nothing.

When Jamie and his mother left to go in the stores, Barkley waited patiently in the car. They had parked in the shade and left the windows down a little so Barkley could stay cool.

Finally they came back carrying four shopping bags full of stuff. But Jamie looked no happier than he did before.

For the next two weeks, Barkley had a few fun times with Jamie. But mostly the summer was dull. Barkley didn't know how much more of this boredom he could stand.

One morning, Barkley woke up as usual and waited for someone to give him his breakfast. He heard Jamie bounding toward the kitchen. Barkley put on his sweetest face and raised his paw. He wanted Jamie to notice him.

But Jamie just ran by him and called, "Bye, Barkley." Then he was out the door and heading down the driveway. Barkley was so surprised he couldn't move fast enough to follow his boy.

Barkley ran to the living room window and looked out. He saw Jamie climb onto a big yellow thing on wheels. It looked like the one his boy always left on when they lived in New York.

That made Barkley very upset because he knew it meant Jamie would be gone all day. He barked and barked, but the big yellow thing moved on down the street.

Mrs. Boggs told Barkley to be quiet and shook her finger at him. Then she went back to clearing the table. The house was so quiet that it gave Barkley the creeps.

When the big yellow thing returned that

afternoon, Barkley was sitting in the front yard waiting. Jamie ran over to the dog and hugged him extra hard. Barkley was thrilled. This was the way things used to be. He wagged his tail to let Jamie know he liked being hugged.

"Hi, how was school?" Mrs. Boggs asked, leaning out the door.

"It was gross," said Jamie. He turned to Barkley. "Do you want a cookie?" The dog wagged his tail eagerly.

Barkley followed Jamie into the kitchen. Jamie pulled a cookie out of the jar and held it over Barkley's head. Just as he had been taught, Barkley cocked his head to the left so that his right ear stood up. He raised his right paw and barked, just once, as if to say "Yes!"

Jamie grinned and said, "Good dog!" He handed over the cookie. "Barkley, I'm sure glad that I have you."

* * *

Every day that week, Mrs. Boggs asked Jamie how school had gone, and every day

Jamie told her it was gross. Finally his mom said, "Well, what seems to be the trouble at school?"

Jamie shrugged. "Well," he began slowly, "at first everybody just stared at me because I'm new. But now this kid named Devon keeps teasing me about Barkley."

"About Barkley?" his mother repeated. "How would this boy know anything about your dog?"

Jamie scuffed one foot against the other. "Oh, he lives on a farm across the woods from us," he explained. "One day Barkley and I went over there by mistake."

"I don't understand why he should tease you about that," said Mrs. Boggs. "The best thing to do is ignore him, and he'll probably forget about it."

* * *

A few days later, the Boggs family was eating supper when Jamie's mom clanked a spoon against her glass. "I have an announcement to make," she said proudly.

The clanking noise scared Barkley, so he went to sit at the other end of the table.

"Guess what," she said. "I just found out I got the job at the real estate office. I'll only be working from nine to three, so I'll be here when you get home from school, Jamie."

"That's great, Mom," said Jamie. "But what about Barkley? You're supposed to be here to take care of him."

"Mothers are people, too," she said firmly. "I thought I'd like staying home by myself, but I like working better. Barkley can stay in the garage until you get home."

Barkley perked his ears when he heard his name. Was it good news? he wondered. Was Jamie going to take him for a walk? Or was he in trouble again?

"He can't stay in the garage," Jamie protested. "It's gross out there."

"He'll be just fine," Mr. Boggs spoke up. "If we try to tie him out back, he always digs holes or gets away. That would be worse."

"But he'll hate the garage," Jamie whined.

"Well, son, it can't be helped this time," said Mr. Boggs. "You know what might happen if Barkley were to run around loose."

"I know," answered Jamie. "The guy with the sheep might hurt Barkley."

Mr. Boggs nodded. "Let's try the garage for now," he said. "We don't want anything to happen to your dog."

The next morning, Mrs. Boggs left even before Jamie was finished dressing for school. His father reminded him to put Barkley in the garage before the school bus came.

Jamie looked down at the dog who lay near his feet. "I'm sorry about this whole mess, Barkley," he said. "I'd be glad to skip school and take care of you. But Mom and Dad would never go for that."

Jamie slowly led the way into the garage. From the tone of his master's voice, Barkley knew whatever was coming was bad. But he wasn't prepared for the garage.

"I know it's pretty crummy in here," said Jamie. "But I brought out your rug. I hope that helps a little." He kneeled down to hug the dog. "You have to stay here. If you run away, you might get into trouble. We might even have to get rid of you, and I couldn't stand that."

Barkley could tell by Jamie's voice that he was upset.

"Jamie, hurry up," Mr. Boggs called from the house. "The bus is coming."

"Okay," the boy answered. "Bye, Barkley." Jamie closed the door behind him.

"Awwwrr!" Barkley protested. But the door stayed closed. He heard the bus pull away and Mr. Boggs's car start. He realized that they weren't coming back to get him out.

Suddenly Barkley had a terrible thought. What if they never came back at all?

"AWWWRR!" he called again. But nobody paid any attention to him. Nobody cares, thought Barkley. If someone did care, Barkley

figured, he wouldn't have to stay out in the garage.

He lay down and put his head on his paws. He whimpered for a long time. But finally he was ready to check the place out. He wanted to see how bad it really was.

The smell of oil hit Barkley's tender nose when he sniffed the cans that lined the floor. Glass jars rocked about when he brushed against the wooden shelf where they sat. A rake fell over and nearly hit him on the head.

Barkley leaped away and ducked beneath an old chair. It was a big wooden thing with space underneath. It looked something like the one Jamie had in his bedroom. Then the dog noticed there was a desk behind the chair he was crouching under.

Barkley loved exploring, so he crawled back under the desk as far as he could get. It seemed like a good place to take a nap, so he curled up in a ball. But after a few minutes his elbows began to hurt from the cold, hard floor.

He scrambled out and sat on his rug. He looked back and forth from his rug to the space he'd been lying in. He wanted the rug in that snug hole, but it looked too big to fit.

Barkley walked back over to the desk and noticed some rags hanging from the wall behind it. He went under the desk and pulled at a rag until it fell at his feet. He made himself a bed. When he was satisfied, he plopped down in the middle.

Now the space was much better. Barkley was pleased with himself. He decided that if he had to stay there, he might as well get comfortable.

# *Three*

When Jamie opened up the big garage door later that afternoon, Barkley was delighted to see him. They played tag and fetch for the rest of the day.

Barkley awoke the next morning and gave Jamie's face a lick. The dog wanted to show his boy that he could be a good sport. Even though he'd been locked up in that awful garage for a whole day, he forgave Jamie.

But once they had both finished their breakfasts, Jamie led Barkley back to the garage again. Barkley was upset. Was he being punished? he wondered. When Jamie left him there, the dog sighed, went to his nest under the desk, and curled up for a nap.

His spot was almost perfect, but it still needed a little more padding, he decided. He reached up and tugged at another rag that hung from the wall. But this one wouldn't budge. Barkley pulled harder and harder. And finally, all at once, a whole wad of cloth came loose. Barkley slammed against the desk. He yelped.

Then he got up and shook himself. He sniffed to make sure he hadn't landed in anything weird. Fresh air hit his nostrils. He looked up to see a hole in the garage wall where the rags had been.

Barkley got on his hind legs and looked out. He could see the woods behind the opening. The hole was pretty big. Could he escape? he wondered.

He shut his eyes to concentrate and squeezed himself into the hole. It was a tight fit, but when he opened his eyes he saw that he was half through. He leaped the rest of the way and rolled out onto the grass. He had done it! He was outside!

Barkley stood up and galloped off in the sunshine. He raced around the house, barking to tell everyone how happy he was. Would someone come to put him back in the garage? he wondered. But no one did.

It felt good to be outside. But what Barkley really wanted was someone to play with. He remembered seeing some kids playing in a sandbox the day he'd gone shopping with Jamie. Barkley thought the kids were nearby, so he went to look for them.

Barkley trotted through long grass and some trees. He found the two little kids running around the front yard of the house next door. Barkley bounded up and stopped. He put on his sweetest look so he wouldn't frighten the kids.

The small boy raced toward Barkley yelling, "Doggie, doggie!"

Barkley wagged his tail and rolled over on

his back. That was a mistake! The boy threw himself on top of Barkley and groped through the dog's fur with sticky fingers. He grabbed Barkley's nose and gave it a twist. That hurt, so Barkley growled.

Then a girl who was even smaller came over. "Puppy!" she screeched, and she fell on Barkley too. She pulled his tail. The dog was scared now. He tried to kick himself free, but the kids were too heavy.

Suddenly Barkley heard a door slam.

"Zachary, Maria, get away from the dirty dog!" a woman's voice screeched. A woman was running toward Barkley with a broom in her hand.

Zachary turned to look at his mother and relaxed his grip. Barkley saw his chance. He squirmed and wiggled himself away from the kids. He raced out of the yard as fast as he could and headed for home.

"Get out of here, you mutt," the woman yelled after him. "And don't ever come back!"

Barkley had had enough for one day. He

galloped to the garage and crawled back inside. He fell asleep almost immediately. But he kept seeing the face of that woman with the broom.

* * *

When Jamie brought Barkley into the house that night, Mrs. Boggs asked, "How was school today, Jamie?"

"Okay, I guess," he answered. "Can I join the 4-H Club? The first meeting is tonight."

"Well, sure, honey," she said looking pleased.

"They have a dog training project," Jamie explained. "I want to show the other kids how smart Barkley really is."

# Four

Right after supper, Jamie went to a shelf in the closet and brought out Barkley's grooming brush. The dog wagged his tail eagerly. He loved to feel the brush's bristles scratch his back.

Jamie sat down on the couch and Barkley sat on the floor in front of him. Jamie always started near Barkley's neck and brushed all the way through his fur. But this time Jamie ran into trouble.

"What's this?" he said, looking at Barkley's neck more closely. "It looks like grape jelly, but where did he get that?"

"I don't know, dear," said his mother. "Must

be something he got into in the garage."

After a while Barkley went for a ride in the car with Jamie and Mrs. Boggs. He was happy about that and bounced around the car as usual. But when they stopped in front of a big building, he began to get suspicious. The building looked a lot like the one where he'd gotten separated from his family in the spring. He didn't want that to happen again.

"Here we are at the fairground," said Mrs. Boggs. "Do you want me to go in with you?"

"No," Jamie said. "The other kids would think I was a sissy." He pulled Barkley out of the car.

"Okay," she agreed. "I'll see you right here at about eight-thirty. Have fun." She waved and drove away.

Jamie sighed and stared at the building. He seemed really worried about going inside, and that made Barkley nervous too. He paced and sat and paced and sat.

Finally a shiny blue car drove up. A girl with a beautiful golden retriever got out. The girl glanced at Jamie, then at Barkley. The dogs touched noses and Barkley wagged his tail.

"Hi," said the girl. "You're new aren't you?"

"Yeah," said Jamie.

"What kind of a dog is that?" she asked.

Jamie looked down at his dog. "I'm not sure," he said. "But his name is Barkley."

"Cute," said the girl. "My dog is named Sadie, and I'm Melissa Taylor. What's your name?"

"Jamie Boggs. I heard about the 4-H Club at school, but I don't know what I'm supposed to do."

Melissa grinned. "No problem," she said. "Just follow me, and I'll get you signed up."

Jamie followed her into the building and Barkley stuck close behind him. The building was really just a steel shell that sat on top of some dirt. The place was so big that Barkley wondered what might be hiding in the corners.

Two women were working on a stack of papers at a small desk. Melissa led Jamie toward them. She stopped in front of the tall, serious woman.

"Mrs. Redding, this is Jamie Boggs," said Melissa.

"And this is Barkley," Jamie added. The woman smiled at Jamie and reached out to the dog. Barkley's tail wagged uncertainly.

"Welcome to our class, Jamie," said the other woman. She seemed more friendly than the first woman. "I'm Mrs. Terrell, and I have some papers here for your parent to sign."

"Can I bring them back next week?" Jamie asked.

"Of course," said Mrs. Terrell. Jamie stuffed the papers into his pocket.

"Jamie, is that the only collar you have for Barkley?" Mrs. Redding asked.

Jamie looked down and shrugged. "Yeah, I guess so."

"You'll need to get one like this," Melissa told him. She worked her fingers under the chain that Sadie wore on her neck. "It's called a choke collar."

"Did you say *choke*?" Jamie asked with a gulp.

"Yes, but don't worry," said Mrs. Terrell. "We use choke collars to give us better control when training the dogs. They don't hurt the dogs."

"Here's how it works," Mrs. Redding explained. She took out a piece of chain with a ring at each end and dropped the chain through one of the rings. Then she slipped the loop she had formed over Barkley's head.

"You tighten this collar when Barkley doesn't pay attention," she said pulling up on the chain.

Barkley wondered what he had done wrong this time. Why had this strange woman put this new thing around his neck? It pulled at his fur when she tugged on it.

He looked around and saw other kids and their dogs arriving. Parents were gathering around to watch. There was noise and confusion as everyone tried to talk at once.

Barkley didn't like so much noise, and he didn't like the new collar. He whined and refused to sit still.

"Maybe you two would like to wait over by the bleachers until we're ready to start," said Mrs. Terrell. "Melissa, will you fill Jamie in on what we'll be doing tonight?"

Melissa nodded and led Sadie toward the bleachers along the side of the building. Jamie and Barkley followed. But suddenly Barkley saw the boy and the German shepherd who lived with the sheep. The big dog growled at Barkley.

"Devon," Melissa said politely, "please tell your dog to back off."

"Why should I?" the boy snapped. "It's that mutt of Jamie's he's after. The one who chases sheep."

"Call your dog off, Devon," she demanded. "Now! Or I'll yell for Mrs. Redding."

Devon shrugged. "Back, Sarge," he said firmly. Instantly, the shepherd stepped to his master's side and was quiet.

Melissa led Jamie and Barkley to a spot near the bleachers. "Wow, that was close," she said.

"Devon's dog could be trouble if Devon won't control him. And he doesn't seem to like you."

"I know," said Jamie. "They live right behind us. Barkley and I went exploring one day and ended up on their property. I thought his dog was going to bite us. His dad warned us to stay away or else."

"Why does he have to be in this class?" Melissa said with a sigh.

"Yeah," said Jamie. "It's going to make things harder for Barkley and me."

"Let's try to forget about him," said Melissa. "I'm supposed to tell you what's going on around here. Here's what I think will happen. We'll split up into two classes. The more advanced kids will work with Mrs. Terrell. The new kids will go with Mrs. Redding."

"You mean I'm not the only beginner?" Jamie asked hopefully.

Melissa grinned. "Nope. I was new last year. This year I'm hoping to win a trophy at the Fall Festival."

"When's that?" asked Jamie.

"Next month," she explained. "There are lots of contests at the festival and a neat little dog show."

"Wow, that sounds great," Jamie said. "If Barkley won something at the show, I'll bet the kids at school would be impressed."

Melissa laughed. "Hold on. You haven't even started training him yet. Besides, the show is only for experienced dog handlers, so you can't enter until next year."

"Rats," Jamie mumbled. "Barkley needs to do something special now."

While the humans talked, Barkley was busy trying to figure out how to get the weird metal collar off. He wanted to meet some of the other dogs and make friends. But he planned to stay a long way away from Devon's shepherd.

Then a pretty white poodle walked by. Barkley definitely wanted to meet her. He thought she was beautiful. Barkley tugged on his leash.

# *Five*

Barkley squirmed away to get closer to the poodle. He thought she was the most beautiful dog he had ever seen. The poodle stared back at Barkley. He wagged his tail cheerfully.

The two instructors tried and tried to get class going. But everyone kept talking, and some of the new dogs started barking at each other. Finally the teachers divided up the kids into two classes.

All the advanced kids took their dogs out to the parking lot with Mrs. Terrell. Barkley saw Melissa and Sadie go with that group. About a dozen dogs remained in the building with Mrs.

Redding. "All right," Mrs. Redding began, "I want you to form a circle around me with your dogs."

Everyone got into a circle. Barkley was right between the fluffy white poodle and a big friendly collie. Right away the collie came over to Barkley and slobbered on him. Barkley pulled away.

"The first thing these dogs must learn is the command *heel*," Mrs. Redding continued. "That means that whenever they walk beside you on the leash, they must keep their noses even with your left leg."

The collie was leaning toward Barkley again. This time Barkley showed his teeth. He didn't like being slobbered on.

"When I say the word *forward*, tell your dog to heel," Mrs. Redding went on. "Start with your left foot and do it just like this. Rover, heel." She started walking with an imaginary dog at her side.

Barkley sensed that something important was about to happen. He wiggled all over.

"Forward," Mrs. Redding commanded.

"Rover, heel," Jamie mumbled, starting forward with his right foot.

Barkley was caught by surprise. Who was Rover? he wondered. And where was everyone going? He braced his feet. When the leash got tight, he pawed at it.

"Hold it!" Mrs. Redding ordered. "Some of you are having a little trouble. Let's all watch and see how my daughter Danielle does it."

Danielle turned out to be the girl with the poodle. She brought her dog to the front.

"Pixie, heel," she said firmly, and away they went, the poodle right at the girl's left leg.

Barkley was impressed, but not by the heeling. He liked that poodle.

"Very good," said Mrs. Redding. "Danielle was in this class last session, but she agreed to help us tonight. Danielle, show them how you turn corners."

Danielle turned to the right and the poodle started past her. The girl slid one hand down

the leash to swing the poodle around.

"See how she holds the leash in her right hand and uses her left to correct the dog?" Mrs. Redding pointed out. "Thank you, dear."

Danielle and the poodle went back to the other dogs. "All right, class. Let's try it again," Mrs. Redding said.

"Barkley, heel," said Jamie, this time remembering to use his left foot.

But Barkley was investigating an interesting scent on the dirt floor just then. He was wondering what kind of animal had made it when there was a yank on his neck.

"Barkley, come on," Jamie urged, pulling harder.

Jamie had never been this rough with Barkley before. It frightened the dog, so he refused to go. A dachshund and the white poodle passed, but Barkley just sat there.

Then he heard a growl. It was Sarge, the German shepherd, and he snapped at Barkley. Barkley leaped forward, almost pulling Jamie off his feet.

Whirling in their direction, Mrs. Redding shouted, "No!" Then she ran over and clapped her hands in the shepherd's face.

"Devon," she said sternly, "you must be more firm with your dog."

"Yes, ma'am," said the boy, and he hauled the shepherd toward him sharply.

Mrs. Redding returned to the middle of the circling dogs. "All right, everyone. Stop!"

Barkley was already stopped, but he moved farther from the shepherd.

"Let's try once more," said Mrs. Redding. "Forward!"

Barkley's eyes were still glued to the shepherd when everyone began to move. He hid behind his boy as the shepherd went by. Jamie fought to keep his feet and kept tugging on Barkley.

After a minute, Mrs. Redding came over and said, "May I try?" She put out her hand, and Jamie gave her the leash.

A powerful right hand shoved Barkley into position. "Barkley, heel," she demanded and surged ahead.

Barkley didn't like Mrs. Redding, so he pulled back. She gave him a series of sharp tugs. That convinced him he really disliked her. Barkley curled up into a ball and was dragged a few steps.

Mrs. Redding stopped, shook her head, and handed the leash back to Jamie. "He's going to be a tough one," she said. "I wish you luck."

When class was finally over, the other kids rushed over to the table with punch and cookies. But Jamie just pulled Barkley to the side and plopped down on the bleachers. He put his head in his hands.

Melissa and Sadie wandered over a few minutes later. Melissa was munching a cookie. "Well, how did it go?" she asked.

Barkley wagged his tail slowly and eyed the cookie. Jamie stared at the floor. "Lousy," he said. "We'll never get it."

"Sure you will," said Melissa. "No one really gets it the first night. Hey, maybe I could come over and help you with Barkley some time."

Jamie sat up then and looked at her. "Would you?" he said. "That would be great."

"Sure," said Melissa. "No problem. Let's go get you some food."

# *Six*

The next morning Barkley went right into the garage without whining. He sprawled on his bed of rags and waited until he heard the car engine whir to life. Then he leaped through the hole in the garage wall, landing lightly on the grass outside.

Barkley ran over to the front lawn and had a nice roll in the grass. Then he started thinking about the pond where he and Jamie had met the sheep. He wanted go swimming, and he was sure he could sneak into the pond without being seen.

Barkley slipped under the fence and then trotted off. A few minutes later, a rabbit popped out in front of him. Barkley rocketed after the rabbit, but it had seen him first and was a few leaps ahead.

Barkley chased the rabbit through the weeds, through a creek, and over a big hill. The rabbit was just inches away when it veered suddenly to the right. Unable to stop, Barkley skidded headfirst into a garden hose.

He jumped to his feet to see where the rabbit had gone. But the garden hose was slithering toward him. It took Barkley a moment to realize that the garden hose had eyes and a long tongue. It was a huge snake that was very much alive!

The snake coiled itself and hissed at him. Barkley jumped into the air and fled as fast as his legs would take him. He ran until he came to another fence, where he stopped to catch his breath.

Finally he looked around. The place looked familiar.

"Scram!" yelled a woman's voice.

Barkley knew he was in trouble. He had run into the yard where the lady with the broom lived, along with her jelly-fingered kids.

The woman charged at Barkley screeching, "You dumb dog. Go away and leave my children alone."

Barkley zoomed off into some tall grass and crouched down to hide. He hoped the lady would leave, but instead she went to the house and returned with her broom. She beat the grass and yelled some more. Barkley had to keep moving to keep from being pounded.

At last the yelling stopped, and he heard footsteps going away. Barkley lay still a little longer just to be on the safe side. Then he crawled off through the long grass.

When he was far enough away from the broom woman, he stood up to shake himself. But suddenly he heard a rustling behind him. He whirled around and came face to face with a very old lady.

She carried a cane above her head like a

club, and for a moment Barkley was too terrified to move. The old lady stood motionless for a moment too. But finally she lowered the cane to her side.

"Oh," she said disgustedly, "it's just another stray dog. The way Susan was yelling, I thought there was something dangerous out here." She turned and began to hobble away. Then she turned back. "Come on," she told Barkley. "You can stay with me until the coast is clear."

Barkley hesitated. Should he go with this strange woman? At least she sounded friendly and looked harmless shuffling along toward her front porch. But she still had that cane. He inched after her, keeping his distance.

The woman went to the porch swing and dropped heavily into it. Barkley sat down a little way away from her and looked around. He realized this was the same old house they had passed on the day he went shopping with Jamie.

"So, what brings you this way, young fella?" Mrs. Williams asked. She said it just as if she were talking to a human.

Barkley wondered what her words meant. She sounded very friendly now, so he wagged his tail and pricked up his ears.

The woman raised her chin and eyed him thoughtfully. "I see," she said. "And what do you think of our president these days?"

Barkley panted a bit. Then he yawned until he squeaked. The woman smiled. "You're quite right," she said.

The morning passed quickly, with Barkley liking the woman's voice more and more. After a while she went into the house. Barkley stood up, too, wondering if he should go.

But in a few minutes, the woman returned carrying two plates. "It's lunchtime," she announced, and she lowered herself carefully into the swing. She set one plate next to her on the swing. She held out the other plate to Barkley.

"Want a sandwich?" she asked.

Barkley understood that question. He sat down, tilted his head, lifted his paw, and said, "Ruff!"

Mrs. Williams laughed. "Well, now, aren't you the smart one?" she said, beaming.

She leaned down to set the second sandwich on the porch floor. When she sat up again, Barkley practically swallowed the sandwich whole.

The woman nibbled her own lunch slowly. Barkley stared at her sandwich and licked his chops. But the woman shook her head.

"That's all for now," she said.

Finished eating at last, she set both plates next to her on the swing. She leaned over and held out her hand.

"Could I pet you?" she asked softly. Her hand reached toward Barkley, and he moved his head to meet it. He loved being petted.

Then the woman began to sniffle. A tear trickled down her wrinkled face. "My boys always had dogs when they lived here," she said. "That was before they married and moved away. It gets awfully lonesome, you know?"

Barkley moved in closer. He poked his head under her hand to encourage her to scratch his head. And she did.

The afternoon zoomed by even faster than the morning had. At last Barkley realized he'd better go home because it was time for Jamie to come. He stood up and took a few steps in that direction.

"Oh, do you have to leave?" Mrs. Williams asked.

Barkley stopped and looked back. Then he turned and headed toward home.

"Please come again soon," the woman called after him.

# Seven

Barkley galloped home and made it back to his bed beneath the desk in plenty of time. When Jamie opened the garage door, Melissa was with him. Barkley was thrilled to have two people to play with. He did a happy dance to let them know how he felt.

"He acts a lot like Sadie," Melissa said with a chuckle. "Dogs have so much personality. You can tell just what they're thinking."

"I'll say," Jamie agreed. "Hi, fella, how was your day?" He scratched Barkley's ears. "Were you bored in here? Let's go get some cookies."

Barkley dashed out the door and headed for the house. The children followed.

"I hope Barkley starts catching on to our lessons," Jamie said. "I don't want to look like a jerk again next week."

"He'll catch on," Melissa said. "He seems smart enough to me."

Jamie went to the cookie jar. He gave a cookie to Melissa and one to Barkley, and grabbed one for himself. Then he took Barkley's leash and new collar down from the shelf in the closet. "So what should we work on first?" he asked.

"Let's go outside and I'll show you," said Melissa.

Jamie led the way to the front door and down the steps. "Here, Barkley. Come on, boy," Jamie called.

Barkley thought the kids wanted to play tag, so he kept just out of Jamie's reach.

"Uh-oh," said Melissa. "He thinks we want to play."

"Wait here," said Jamie. "I'll get another cookie." He raced into the house and returned waving a cookie. "Here, Barkley. Want a cookie?"

Barkley pricked up his ears. He ran to get

his treat. But as Jamie handed him the cookie, Melissa slipped the choke collar over his head.

While Barkley wondered why, Jamie stood in the position he had learned in class. Melissa patted Barkley on the head to encourage him.

"Okay, Barkley, heel," said Jamie.

Barkley was angry. He wondered why Jamie, his favorite person in the whole world, kept doing weird things to him. Jamie had asked if he wanted a cookie, and now Jamie was yanking on his neck. It wasn't fair.

Barkley planted his feet. Jamie pulled sharply on the leash. Barkley lay down and refused to move.

"I don't understand this," said Melissa. "I mean, Sadie never acted this way. Let me try."

"Wait, I've got it," said Jamie. "We need more cookies. If anything will get Barkley moving, it's food."

Sure enough, when Jamie dangled food in front of him, Barkley went forward with Melissa. But he didn't really understand what

they were trying to teach him.

As soon as Barkley got his cookie, he sat down again. Melissa tried to keep him going, but Barkley paid no attention. She hauled on the leash. He pulled back.

"Wow, he's strong when he wants to be," she complained.

"Let me take him," said Jamie. "You can handle the cookies."

"I don't think Mrs. Redding would approve of this," Melissa said as they switched places. "If you try sneaking him cookies in class, you might have a stampede on your hands."

"Do you have any better ideas?" asked Jamie.

"No," she admitted.

"Okay, then we'll do it my way for now," said Jamie. He gave Melissa his cookies, and she walked to a place about ten feet in front of Barkley. She held out a cookie.

"Barkley, heel," said Jamie, starting forward.

The dog lunged toward the cookie, dragging Jamie with him. Jamie yanked on the leash with all his might and yelled, "Barkley, heel." Barkley dropped back to Jamie's speed.

"He did it," Jamie cheered as they reached Melissa and Barkley claimed his reward.

They tried again and again until Barkley could heel perfectly. Then all three of them collapsed in a heap.

"He's got it," said Jamie. "Wait until the rest of the class sees us!"

"Yeah, he's got it for now," said Melissa. "But there won't be any cookies in class. What will you do to get Barkley's attention then?"

Jamie shrugged. "I'll keep working with him," he said. "Maybe he won't need cookies by the time we have our next class. Can you come over again tomorrow night?"

Melissa nodded. "Sure, I'll be here," she said. "I wouldn't want to let you and Barkley down."

\* \* \*

The next morning Barkley crawled through the hole in the garage the minute Jamie left on the bus. He set out for Mrs. Williams's house immediately.

He found her sitting on her front porch swing and humming to herself. She stopped humming when she spotted him.

"Oh, there you are," she said, just as if she'd been expecting him. "I'm so glad you could come. I wanted to show you my flowers."

The old woman took a long time to get up off the swing and position her cane in front of her. She leaned heavily on the cane as she hobbled across the porch and down the three steps to the sidewalk. Shuffling through the overgrown grass, she finally stopped at a weedy patch of purple and yellow flowers.

"Aren't they pretty?" she asked, pointing down. "I can't take care of them like I should anymore, but a few of them come up every year."

The woman shuffled on, pointing to things as she went along. Barkley liked the sound of her voice, and she seemed happy to have him along. He followed her all around the yard, then back to her porch swing.

Later she went inside and came back with sandwiches. Just like the day before, Barkley gulped his down in a hurry.

After lunch, they each took a long nap. But a loud thump woke Barkley. Glancing around, he saw that the woman's cane had fallen.

"Ruff, ruff," Barkley said, to let her know what had happened.

Mrs. Williams sat up slowly. She looked down at the cane and began to squirm. "Oh my," she said. "I'll have to get that back, but it's so hard for me to reach things on the floor."

Barkley wanted to help. He went over to the cane and picked it up in his mouth. Then he waddled over to the woman and held up the cane so that she could reach it. He waited until she got a good grasp on it, then let go.

Mrs. Williams gave a delighted giggle. "Oh, you are such a wonderful dog," she gushed. "I can't believe how smart you are. Why, you're just as smart as a person."

Barkley wagged his tail and ducked his head

in embarrassment. He loved being praised, but he didn't want to look too proud of himself. When she had finished talking, he jumped off the porch and brought her a stick.

"I'll bet you want me to throw this," she said with a grin. Barkley danced around and moved away from her to be ready for her toss.

"All right, here it comes," she called, throwing the stick as hard as she could. It landed about two feet from the porch, and Barkley quickly brought it back.

"Oh, what fun," she giggled. "Try to get this one."

She threw the stick again, and this time it went a little farther. Barkley brought it back to her. They had a great time until Barkley remembered Jamie would be coming home soon. The dog sat at the woman's feet for a moment so she could pet him again. Then he trotted away.

"Will I see you tomorrow?" she called after him. He barked and jumped from side to side to answer her.

# Eight

On Friday afternoon, Barkley lay on his bed in the garage and groaned. His belly was killing him.

He heard the bus come and then Jamie walking up to the garage door. But Barkley felt too awful to even get to his feet.

The garage door opened, and there stood Jamie. "Hey, Barkley, I'm home. It's Friday! Yeah!"

Barkley raised his head and gave Jamie a sad look. Jamie tried again. "Barkley, I'm home. Get up."

The dog struggled to his feet. But it was no use. He fell back again and whimpered.

"Barkley, what's wrong?" Jamie gasped. "Are you sick?"

The dog knew he was scaring Jamie, but he couldn't help it. Mrs. Williams had made three pans of raisin cookies, and she'd given Barkley all he wanted. He had eaten too many cookies.

"Hey, Barkley, want a cookie?" Jamie asked. The dog shut his eyes and gave a mighty groan.

"Boy, you must be sick," said Jamie.

Just then Mrs. Boggs drove up in her car. Jamie raced over to her yelling, "Mom, Mom, Barkley's sick."

Mrs. Boggs come to the garage and looked down at Barkley. "Hmm," she said. "He does look sick, but I don't have time to take him to the veterinarian. I'm going to an important meeting tonight. Your father should be home soon. He can help you." Then she hurried off toward the house.

Jamie picked up Barkley and half dragged, half carried the dog to his bedroom. The boy put the dog in the middle of his own bed. He covered him with a blanket. Jamie's bed felt wonderful and Barkley fell asleep.

The sound of Mr. Boggs's car woke Barkley. He slowly stood up on the bed and realized his stomachache was gone. He jumped off the bed and ran to find Jamie. His boy was in the kitchen talking to Mr. Boggs.

"Ruff, ruff," Barkley said happily. He went over and put his head underneath Jamie's hand to be petted.

Jamie looked down and grinned. "Gee, Dad, I guess he's okay," said the boy. "I thought Barkley was really sick. He wouldn't eat a cookie or anything."

"Well, he looks fine now," said Mr. Boggs. "But keep your eye on him tonight just to be sure."

* * *

The next Tuesday night, Barkley got into the car with Jamie, and they headed for their second dog-training class.

"I hope you do good this time," Jamie told

him. "I hate having everyone laugh at us."

When they got to the class, Barkley was glad to see Melissa. She always seemed to have cookies. He even tried to follow her and Sadie to their class, but Jamie held him back.

Mrs. Redding went to the front of the room and said, "All right, class. This time I want you to get your dogs into the sitting position before you tell them to heel. Then be sure your dog sits again each time you stop walking."

Barkley was still looking around for Melissa. When Jamie asked him to sit, Barkley ignored him.

"Barkley, I said SIT," Jamie declared in a louder voice. He pushed hard against the dog's rear end.

Barkley thought this was weird, so he pulled away and jumped up on his hind legs. Jamie pushed him back down to the floor.

"Barkley, sit!" Jamie ordered, and he wrestled with the dog. Barkley loved to wrestle. He fought back with all four legs and licked

Jamie's face whenever he could reach it.

Suddenly Mrs. Redding appeared above them. "Here, let me help you," she said, grabbing Barkley's leash.

From the sound of her voice, Barkley knew she meant business. He froze with fear, then tried to get to Jamie for protection. But Mrs. Redding quickly yanked the dog to the ground. He whimpered as she pushed him into a sitting position. Jamie's eyes grew big watching them.

"Don't worry," said Mrs. Redding. "I didn't hurt him. When Barkley tries to jump up on you, you should get him in the chest with your knee. If he won't sit, use the point of your thumb on his rear end. Understand?"

"Uh, sure," Jamie mumbled, and he took Barkley's leash back from her.

Mrs. Redding returned to her spot at the head of the group. "Okay, everyone, forward!" she called out.

Barkley looked at her and growled softly. "Barkley, heel," Jamie said loudly. He jerked on the leash and his voice was stern. This time Barkley listened and obeyed.

"That's much better, Jamie," Mrs. Redding called. "Okay, everybody. Halt!"

Jamie stopped walking, but Barkley kept going. He'd finally figured out that was what he was supposed to do.

"Sit!" Jamie said firmly. When Barkley didn't, the boy pushed down with his thumb near the dog's tail. Barkley sat.

"Good dog," Jamie squealed, and he leaned down to give Barkley a pat on the head. Barkley was so thrilled to be praised that he leaped up to lick Jamie's face.

"Oh, no," Jamie moaned. "Barkley, cool it. Everyone's looking at us." Barkley caught the tone of Jamie's voice and sat back down.

The next time Barkley heeled right away and sat as soon as Jamie told him to. Jamie patted the dog's head and praised him. The room got noisy with everyone talking to the dogs.

Mrs. Redding clapped her hands together.

"Okay, gang, let's spread out into a big circle. We're going to learn some new things tonight."

All of the dogs sniffed at each other as their owners pulled them into position. Barkley felt safe where he was, so he didn't want to move. But suddenly the playful collie was coming at him. Horrified, Barkley watched as the huge hairy dog come bounding toward him. He ducked out of the collie's way just in time.

Barkley tried to run, but his leash was stuck underneath the collie. Both Jamie and the collie's owner pulled frantically on their leashes, but it didn't help. Soon all four bodies were tangled into a crazy, mangled mess.

"Hobo, please get up," pleaded the collie's owner.

"Barkley," Jamie wailed.

Then Mrs. Redding appeared, and the other kids and their dogs gathered around to watch.

"Look," a boy called out. "It's that dumb dog of Jamie's again. That dog can't do anything right."

Mrs. Redding ignored the boy. She reached over to Barkley and unhooked the leash from his collar. She picked up the dog and handed him to Jamie. Grabbing the collie's leash, she helped it to its feet.

"Okay, now," she said. "Please watch your dogs more carefully. Don't let them get too close to each other, or we'll spend the whole class straightening out messes. Let's get back to work."

Class passed quickly and Barkley didn't get yelled at again. He saw Melissa again, but she didn't have any cookies. He was disappointed.

# Nine

When they pulled up at the fairground the following Tuesday night, Barkley could sense that Jamie was extra nervous. Before they got out of the car, the boy pulled the dog's face even with his own and made Barkley look him in the eye.

"Barkley," he said, "you've just got to get things right tonight. Melissa and I have practiced and practiced with you. If you don't get it this time, you're hopeless."

They went into the building, and the instructors divided the classes as usual. Mrs. Redding told them to get into a big circle again, facing her.

Barkley saw to his horror that Devon and Sarge were on his left. He leaned in closer to Jamie's leg and looked longingly at the sweet-looking cocker spaniel on Jamie's other side.

"Class," said Mrs. Redding, "tonight we're going to teach your dogs to stay. When I tell you to walk away from your dogs, be sure they are sitting flat on the floor. You'll wave your hand in front of your dog's face and say *stay*. Then leave, starting with your right foot."

While Mrs. Redding talked on and on, the German shepherd edged slowly toward Barkley. Barkley wished Jamie would look back and see what was happening, but his boy was too interested in what the instructor was saying. Sarge was just inches away now, wearing a nasty grin.

When Barkley could stand it no longer, he moved around to Jamie's right side. But still Sarge inched closer and closer.

Suddenly Devon looked down. "No," he said, and he yanked Sarge back into position.

Jamie took a step away from Sarge and pulled Barkley back to his left side. Barkley leaned into Jamie's leg.

Mrs. Redding spoke again. "Okay, everyone tell your dog to stay, and walk toward the center of the circle until you come to the end of your leash. Then turn to face your dog and wait. When I tell you to go back, return and praise your dog. Do you have all that?"

Everyone nodded.

"Fine," she said. "Then let's make the circle bigger and try it."

Soon there was a loud chorus of "Stay," and Barkley saw a hand pass in front of his eyes. Jamie was walking away, and the German shepherd looked ready to attack at any moment. Barkley was sure that if he stayed where he was, he would be eaten.

Barkley dashed after his boy. But Jamie looked back and groaned.

"No, Barkley," he cried.

Barkley knew he'd done something wrong

again, but he didn't know what. He cringed as Jamie dragged him back to the starting place.

The boy spoke firmly to him. "This time you're going to stay. Do you understand?"

Jamie tried the stay command again, and again Barkley followed him.

"Okay, return to your dogs now and give them some praise," said Mrs. Redding.

Jamie just stood there. Barkley saw all the other dogs being petted and hugged, but Jamie wouldn't even look down. Barkley felt awful.

Next the class practiced the heel command for a while, and Barkley did better. Then they returned to the new lesson. "Stay," said the chorus of kids.

Barkley ignored the rest of the class and stayed as close to Jamie's leg as he could.

"No," pleaded Jamie. "Get back there."

At last Mrs. Redding said, "Everyone practice your stay command this week. Next week, you'll be walking farther from your dogs, and they'll have to wait longer before you come back. Now, before we finish tonight, I'd like to try one more thing. When I say *fast*, I want you to run with your dog. Make your dog work to keep up with you. When I say *slow*, just creep along.

"Okay, fast!" Mrs. Redding shouted.

Suddenly the whole class began to race around. Barkley loved it. "Ruff," he said, dancing sideways. "Ruff, ruff."

Some of the other dogs started dancing like Barkley. Soon all the dogs were barking and prancing. Barkley noticed the German shepherd staring at him. He saw a determined look in the other dog's eyes.

"Grrr," said the big dog as he leaped at Barkley.

Barkley panicked. He needed a place to hide—and fast. The first place he saw was the refreshment table.

Two mothers were busy laying plates of cookies and brownies on the table. A huge bowl of purple punch and some gooey doughnuts sat on the table, too.

Barkley shot toward the table with the German shepherd in hot pursuit. Their boys were hauled along behind them. The cookies the women were holding shot into the air as the women took off in opposite directions. One of the doughnuts landed on an Irish setter's head and another stuck to the wall. The flying cookies and doughnuts were attacked by ten hungry dogs.

The punch landed everywhere, making a goopy, gloppy, purple mess on the floor. Danielle's white poodle now had a purple stripe down its back. Sarge had a soaked head. He lay in the middle of all the craziness licking purple punch off the floor.

Barkley didn't stop to eat. He raced to a corner of the room and stood there shaking. He looked back to see Jamie sprawled across the floor. Sarge was still licking punch, so Barkley went over to Jamie and licked the boy's face.

Jamie groaned and said, "Barkley, you're hopeless. I'm never coming back here again."

"Hold it," Mrs. Redding demanded. "Who started all of this?"

Devon jumped to his feet, wiping punch from his face with his sleeve. "It was that stupid dog of Jamie's," he said. "He's the one to blame."

Jamie stood up too. "No, it wasn't Barkley's fault," he said, glaring at Devon. "Your dog took after mine. Sarge was chasing Barkley."

"He was not!"

"He was too," Jamie insisted.

"Boys, stop it," ordered Mrs. Redding. "What's done is done. Let's have everyone just sit down and calm down for a few minutes."

Devon and Jamie eyed each other angrily as they pulled their dogs to opposite ends of the bleachers.

Mrs. Redding took a few deep breaths and crossed her arms. "At least this class is never dull," she said. "Now what did I want to tell you? Oh, yes, I have some special news about the Fall Festival dog show. This year the festival committee has added a class just for beginners."

"Yeah!" the kids cheered.

"That's the good news," she continued. "The bad news is that we have only one more training session before the show. Mrs. Terrell and I have to go to a meeting the following Tuesday."

A gasp of disbelief went up.

"How do we enter?" asked Devon.

Mrs. Redding gave them all the details and handed out entry blanks. When Jamie reached for one, Devon shot him a nasty look.

"You're not going to enter that dumb dog of yours, are you?" he sneered.

"Yes, I am," said Jamie. "Do you have a problem with that?"

"Your stupid dog will wreck the whole show," Devon said with a snort.

"Not if your creepy dog stays out of his way," Jamie replied. "He's always picking on Barkley. Just keep him away from us, and my dog will do fine."

Devon look over at Mrs. Redding, who was

eyeing them. He turned and dragged Sarge in the other direction.

Soon Melissa came up. "Hey, did you hear the good news?" she asked. "The festival has added a division for beginners. That means you and Barkley can enter the dog show."

"Yeah, I heard," said Jamie. "But I'm not so sure I can train Barkley in time."

"We'll do it," said Melissa. "I'll help you every day. We're a team now. Right?"

"Right," said Jamie. "It's neat to have a friend."

# Ten

Melissa came over the next night. She told Jamie what to do, and he had Barkley heel all over the place. They went forward at regular speed, then fast, then slow. They made right turns and left turns. They even did figure eights. Barkley stayed right at Jamie's left leg.

"Good dog, Barkley. You're doing great!" cried Jamie, hugging his dog.

"He sure is," said Melissa. "Let's try to teach him to stay."

Jamie had Barkley sit and told him to stay. But Barkley knew what Jamie really wanted. He knew it made Jamie happy if he stayed right next to the boy's left leg. Barkley caught up to Jamie and wagged his tail.

"No, Barkley, you're supposed to stay," Jamie said unhappily.

"I'll hold him this time to give him the idea," Melissa offered.

"Okay," said Jamie. He put Barkley in position again and said, "Stay."

Barkley started to get up, but Melissa held him down. He liked Melissa, so he stayed with her. Soon Jamie came back and praised him. Barkley was pleased.

"Now try it without me," she said, standing back to watch.

"Stay," said Jamie, waving his hand in Barkley's face. Barkley scampered right after him.

They tried it again and again, but each time Barkley tried to go with Jamie. Then Melissa had to rush in, yell "Stay," and drag Barkley back to his special spot. Nobody offered Barkley any cookies.

On the ninth try, Melissa said, "This isn't working. We need something to make him sit the minute he tries to get up."

"Yeah," Jamie agreed. "But what?"

They sat down on the porch to think. Barkley sat down, too.

After a while, Jamie said, "How about a squirt gun?"

Melissa frowned, then smiled. "Yeah," she said. "It just might work. Do you have one around?"

"I think so," said Jamie. "Come on." They ran into the house and Jamie led the way to his room. Barkley stayed close behind, wondering what game they would play next.

Jamie opened his closet door and began to toss things out. "Ah, here it is," he said. He handed the bright green squirt gun to Melissa. "You get to be the shooter."

They hurried back out to the kitchen and ran some water into the gun. Then the kids dashed back out the door with Barkley in hot pursuit. Melissa stood off to one side with the green gun and waited.

Jamie made Barkley sit next to him.

"Barkley, stay," he said. Flashing the hand signal, he walked off. Barkley was on his feet immediately, but he was in for a surprise.

*Splat!* A stream of water hit Barkley in the nose. He was so surprised, he sat right back down.

"Yahoo, it worked!" Jamie cheered and started jumping around the yard. Barkley was so happy to have done something right that he got up and started bouncing around too.

"Barkley," wailed Melissa, "you're not supposed to move yet."

She pointed the squirt gun at the dog and pulled the trigger. But only a few drops of water trickled out of the gun. Barkley made it safely to Jamie and nudged his hand to be petted.

"Jamie," Melissa scolded, "that was your fault. You're not supposed to jump up and down. You're supposed to stand still and look grouchy until the command is over."

"Sorry," said Jamie sheepishly. "Can we try it again?"

"Sure," said Melissa, "as soon as I reload."

Melissa ran back in the house and put more water into the gun. When she came back outside, Jamie put Barkley in position and told him to stay. When he tried to get up, Melissa squirted him with water again. Jamie repeated the stay command. The dog was starting to get the idea, but he had to try to get up once more.

*Splat!* That did it. From then on, Barkley stayed put whenever Jamie told him to stay.

\* \* \*

That night at dinner, Jamie told his parents about his new method of dog training. "And I have even bigger news," he went on.

"What's that?" his dad asked.

"There's a dog show at the Fall Festival, and they have a class for beginners. I want to be in it."

"Are you sure that's what you want?" his mother asked.

"Yes," said his father. "For weeks you've been telling us how badly Barkley's been doing in class. What if he won't cooperate in this dog show?"

"We'll be okay," Jamie said confidently.

"Melissa and I have worked hard with him, and we'll keep right on working until the day of the dog show."

"Okay, as long as you don't get your heart set on winning," said Mr. Boggs.

"Yes, just do your best," Mrs. Boggs agreed. "Remember that dog training should be fun."

"Sure, Mom," said Jamie. "But it would be extra fun to win."

"I'm proud of you for sticking with this," said Mr. Boggs.

"Yes," said Mrs. Boggs. "We know that Barkley hasn't been an easy dog to train."

"We've both learned a lot," said Jamie.

\* \* \*

At class the following Tuesday night, Mrs. Redding looked really surprised when Jamie told her he wanted to enter Barkley in the dog show.

"Do you think there's any use?" she asked.

"Sure," Jamie told her. "I've been working really hard with him, and he's starting to catch on."

"But Jamie, you have to admit he's never

behaved very well with other dogs," she said, shaking her head. "If he doesn't shape up tonight, I doubt he will listen to you at the show."

"He'll be better, you'll see," Jamie insisted.

Mrs. Redding smiled politely and rolled her eyes. But Barkley really did understand what Jamie wanted now. He heeled like a champ, and even when *stay* lasted longer than usual, he waited patiently for Jamie to tell him to move.

Mrs. Redding came up to Jamie when class was over. "I see you really have been working with him," she said. "You're some dog trainer."

"Yeah," said the girl with the collie. "He was a million times better than last week."

"Thanks," said Jamie. "Melissa's been helping us. I hope he does this well at the show."

* * *

Melissa and Jamie worked with Barkley every night. Some nights Melissa brought Sadie along so they could get in some practice, too. She told Jamie how excited she was about entering the advanced division.

Whenever Sadie came along, Barkley felt like showing off for her. When it was his turn to perform, he tried to do the very best he could. He loved the way Jamie squealed with delight when Barkley did something right. The dog had decided he liked dog training after all.

But each morning, Barkley still slipped out of the garage and ran over to Mrs. Williams's house. Having her for a friend was very special to him.

One day Mrs. Williams even fed Barkley a big, juicy hamburger. She also brought out an old piece of carpeting for him to take his nap on. After their naps, they usually took a walk around the yard and looked at her flowers. She was always waiting for him on her porch when he got there.

Then came the morning that Mrs. Williams wasn't waiting on her porch. She usually shared her breakfast with Barkley, but where was she?

The dog went up on the porch and sniffed

the swing. He could tell the old woman hadn't been there yet this morning. Barkley trotted around back to the flower bed, but she wasn't there either. He returned to the porch and looked in the front window. Still he didn't see her.

Something had to be wrong, Barkley decided. But what? And what should he do? He had no idea where Jamie or Mr. and Mrs. Boggs were. And if he went looking for them, he might get lost like he had when they moved to Indiana. No, he didn't want that!

"Ruff," Barkley said loudly, pawing at the door. But Mrs. Williams didn't come. He tried barking at the back door too. There was no answer.

Puzzled and frightened, Barkley went to the back window. He jumped up on his hind legs and looked into the kitchen. There was Mrs. Williams! She was lying flat on the floor, and she wasn't moving.

"Ruff, ruff, ruff!" Barkley said frantically. He

had to get inside the house. He had to wake her up. He had to see if she was okay.

Barkley ran around and around the house. He looked for an open window that he could squeeze through, but they were all shut tight.

His head spun. He had to save Mrs. Williams. Next to Jamie, she was Barkley's best friend. He just had to help her.

He howled in frustration and ran out to the road. If only Jamie or his parents would drive up, he thought. But the road was empty.

Again he ran to the back window and looked in. Mrs. Williams was still there, and she still hadn't moved. He ran to the road and looked down it again. There were no cars, no sign of life.

Then suddenly Barkley knew what he had to do. He took off through the long grass at full speed.

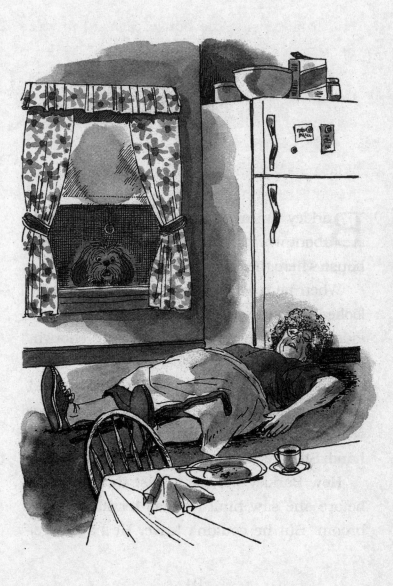

# Eleven

Barkley ran on and on, trying not to think about what lay ahead. He was going to the house where the broom woman lived.

When he reached the edge of her lawn, he looked both ways. He hoped her jelly-fingered kids were somewhere else, and sure enough, the coast was clear.

Barkley ran swiftly across the lawn and peeked in the window. He could see the broom woman standing there with a telephone in her hand. She was looking the other way.

How Barkley wanted to just turn and run before she saw him! He was terrified of her broom. But he couldn't leave. He had to get help for Mrs. Williams.

He got as close to the window as he could. "Ruff, ruff," he barked.

The broom woman swung around quickly. Barkley could see the anger in her face. Every part of him said, "Run! She'll get you for sure." But Barkley didn't run. In fact, he barked again.

Eyes flashing, the woman slammed down the phone and grabbed her broom. She burst out the front door of the house.

"You dumb dog!" she screamed. "What are you doing back here? I'll get you this time."

Barkley backed up, but he didn't run. He barked twice more and stood his ground. How could he make her see that this was serious? How could he tell her about Mrs. Williams?

"Get out of here," the woman bellowed as she swung her broom through the air.

Barkley kept right on barking, bouncing up and down with the effort.

"I will not stand for this," she said. "You have no right to bother me. No right at all!" She took a step closer to Barkley and swung hard. Barkley dodged just in time.

She swung again, but Barkley ducked and ran a little way away. The next time the woman swung, he darted in to grab the end of the broom with his teeth. He held on with all his strength.

"That does it," the woman yelled angrily. "I'm calling the sheriff to come and get you."

Barkley tugged at the broom so hard that a piece of it came off in his teeth. The woman's eyes flashed with anger, and she kicked at him. Barkley galloped over to the edge of her lawn and waited, grinning at her. He dared her to catch him.

The broom woman chased after him, swinging wildly. Barkley danced ahead of her, and waited again. When she got close, he darted away again.

"Oh, I give up," she said. "I can't catch you." She turned to go. But Barkley zoomed around so he was in front of her again and got her

back on his trail.

As they neared Mrs. Williams's house, the broom woman started screaming. "Myrtle, this dog is crazy! Call the sheriff! Call him now!"

Barkley wondered if her screams would wake Mrs. Williams. He ran up to the porch and barked as loudly as he could. He had to show the broom lady where Mrs. Williams was.

The broom woman leaned against the porch pillars, trying to catch her breath. Barkley jumped off the porch and gave three quick yelps to signal her to follow him.

Instead, the woman glared at him and called, "Myrtle, are you in there? Call the sheriff, I tell you."

The woman climbed the porch steps and knocked on the front door. She waited a minute and tried to open it. When she couldn't, she followed Barkley around to the back. She knocked again, then tried to open that door. It wouldn't open either.

Barkley jumped at the kitchen window and

barked some more. Finally the woman caught on. She peered through the window and her eyes widened.

"Good heavens!" she said. "Poor Myrtle."

The broom lady slammed her body against the door, but it still didn't open. She tried again, and the door creaked but held. She found an old board propped up against the house and used it to charge the door. The rickety old wood caved in at last.

Barkley was in the door in a flash. He licked Mrs. Williams's face. He could tell she was alive. The broom woman put her head up to Mrs. Williams's mouth. She held Mrs. Williams's wrist for a few seconds.

Then the woman ran to the phone and dialed. Barkley stayed with Mrs. Williams and licked her hand to tell her help was coming. He hoped she would be all right. He wanted to hear her sweet voice again. He wanted her to give him treats and throw sticks for him to fetch. She just had to get better.

A little while later, Barkley heard a strange wailing sound. He saw flashing lights, and the broom woman ran to the front door. When she opened it, two men ran inside.

"Boy, am I glad to see you," said the broom woman. "She definitely needs an ambulance."

"Where is she?" one of the men asked.

"Back in the kitchen," said the broom woman, leading the way. "It looks as if she fell. She's unconscious, and I think she has a broken leg."

The two men checked on Mrs. Williams. "You're right," said the second man. "She's pretty banged up, and her leg is broken."

The first man was poking Mrs. Williams with some metal things. He looked up. "Who are you?" he asked. "Are you a relative?"

"Oh, no, I'm just a neighbor," said the broom lady. "I hardly ever come over here. But today this crazy dog showed up at my house. He wouldn't leave me alone, so I chased him with my broom. We ended up here, and I found her like this."

The man smiled a big smile. "Wow," he said. "That's quite a story. I don't think this dog is crazy at all. In fact, I'd say he's a big-time hero. This poor old lady could have lain here for a long time if he hadn't gotten you to follow him."

The broom woman's mouth dropped open, and she stared at Barkley. "What?" she said. "Do you really think this dog led me here on purpose?"

"Sure," said the man. "It wouldn't be the first time a dog was smart enough to do something like this."

Barkley saw that the look in the woman's eyes had changed. He couldn't keep from wagging his tail. He was so happy that these people were helping Mrs. Williams. He thought she would be all right again soon.

The two men carefully put Mrs. Williams on a long bed on wheels. They put her in a car with a flashing light on top. Barkley heard the loud wailing sound again, and the car zoomed away.

Barkley wondered where they were taking

his friend. He hoped it was some place nice. He hoped she would be back soon and be all better. He looked up at the broom lady and cautiously wagged his tail. He wanted to thank her for getting help for Mrs. Williams.

To Barkley's surprise, she smiled at him. "I was wrong about you," she said. She knelt to pat his head. "And I'm really sorry for the way I treated you. From now on you can play with Zach and Maria whenever you want."

Barkley couldn't understand her words, but he could tell she liked him a lot better than before. And that was good enough for him.

"Ruff, ruff," he replied.

# Twelve

About a week later, Jamie woke Barkley up early. He got a very small breakfast and a very long bath. Next Jamie used a noisy hair dryer, his regular brush, and a special comb on Barkley. What a way to start the day!

Then Jamie went to his room and put on a pair of new white jeans and a bright green T-shirt that said "4-H." Mrs. Boggs packed food and Mr. Boggs packed drinks. Barkley knew something big was about to happen. He hoped it had nothing to do with airplanes.

At last they all piled into the car and headed off to the fairground. When they got to the place where Barkley and Jamie usually practiced, everything looked different. There were cars, tents, people, and strange animals everywhere. The wonderful smells of cotton candy, caramel corn, French fries, hamburgers, and all those strange animals filled the air. Noisy music and loud yelling hurt Barkley's ears.

At first the dog just wanted to go back to the car. But then he saw other dogs and kids having fun. He walked very slowly, trying to see everything.

Soon Barkley felt Jamie tugging on his leash. He looked up to see his boy's eyes fixed on a small roped-off arena where lots of kids and dogs were gathering. A sign said "Dog Show . . . 2:00 p.m."

Barkley saw the super friendly collie and the cocker spaniel from class. He wagged his tail and pulled Jamie toward them. But then Barkley saw that Sarge and Devon were there too, and he hesitated.

"I sure hope Barkley remembers everything I taught him," Jamie told his parents.

"Don't worry," said Mr. Boggs. "You've done your best, and we'll be proud of you no matter what happens."

"I know, but I'm nervous," said Jamie.

"It's almost two o'clock," said Mrs. Boggs. "Don't you think you should go over with the other kids?"

"Yeah," said Jamie, reaching down to adjust Barkley's collar. "But Devon's over there. I hate to stand near him any longer than necessary."

Jamie took a deep breath and headed toward the roped-off arena. Barkley stiffened. "Barkley, heel," said Jamie, and Barkley moved up next to Jamie's leg. Then they were face to face with the German shepherd.

Barkley cringed and the two boys glared at each other. "Why did you have to show up?" Devon sneered.

"Why did you?" Jamie shot back.

"Because Sarge is going to win, that's why," Devon snapped.

"Oh, yeah? Want to bet?" Jamie replied.

Mrs. Redding suddenly appeared behind them. "Boys, that's enough," she said. "Stop arguing right now or I'll have you both disqualified from the dog show."

The boys said no more, but they continued to give each other dirty looks. And Sarge growled low in his throat.

Just then Barkley spotted Melissa and Sadie. He dragged Jamie toward them. Melissa was peering into her dog's throat.

"What are you doing?" asked Jamie. "Is something the matter?"

"No," said Melissa. "I was just checking Sadie's teeth to be sure they were clean. Every detail is important in a 4-H show."

Jamie's eyes grew big. "So are they clean enough?" Jamie wondered. "What about Barkley's teeth? Are they okay? Will you help me check?"

Barkley wondered what they were talking about because his boy sounded very worried.

"Sadie's are fine," said Melissa, letting her

dog's mouth go. Then she took hold of Barkley's mouth. He was too surprised to resist when she pulled his jaws open and looked in.

"Phew!" she said, making a face. "Didn't you brush his teeth?"

"Well, no," said Jamie, his voice raising in pitch. "I didn't know I was supposed to."

Melissa laughed. "You should see your face," she said. "I was just teasing you."

Jamie frowned, and then he laughed too. "Oh," he said. "You really had me going there."

"Relax," Melissa giggled. "I only did that because you looked so miserable. Smile. This is going to be fun, and Barkley will do fine."

"I hope so," said Jamie.

Soon a man in a straw hat appeared with a microphone. "Ladies and gentlemen," he said. "May I have your attention, please? We're about to start our 4-H Fair dog show. And our first class is for beginner handlers."

"That's you," said Melissa, giving Jamie a gentle shove.

Jamie and Barkley joined the rest of the kids and the dogs that had been in their dog training class.

"When I call your name," said the man, "you will sit your dog at the entrance to the arena. When I say go, you will heel to the first corner, turn left, speed up for about six steps, and walk normally again."

"That's easy," Jamie muttered softly. "I don't know why I was so worried."

But Barkley's ear itched. So he sat down and began to scratch it. Jamie looked down and frowned. He swatted Barkley's paw to make him stop.

"Next, do a halt, turn the second corner, then do a slow heel, go back to normal speed, go around the third corner, and stop again just inside the entrance. We'll do the sit-stays as a group at the end."

Jamie gulped. "Oops," he muttered. "I spoke

too soon. That's a lot to remember, for both of us."

"Any questions?" the announcer said. The kids exchanged panicky looks, but no one said anything.

"All right, then," said the man. "Let's start with Jamie Boggs and Barkley."

Jamie gasped. He looked down at Barkley and then over at his parents. They waved encouragingly.

"Are you ready, Jamie?" the announcer asked.

"Uh, sure," Jamie said weakly. "Come on, Barkley. I didn't want to be first. But you'll remember what we practiced, won't you? This is your big chance to be a star."

Barkley felt a light tug on his leash, and he followed Jamie to the edge of the arena. He could tell that Jamie was afraid. He wondered if Jamie knew that something bad was waiting for them in the arena. Barkley decided to check everything out just in case.

He sniffed at the ropes around the arena. He eyed the judge and the announcer. They both looked kind of weird. Yes, he would keep an eye on them.

"Sit," said Jamie. But Barkley knew this was no time for sitting. He had to watch for trouble.

"Sit," the boy repeated. Barkley squirmed and gave him a frustrated look. He felt Jamie's thumb on his behind, and sat. But he was ready to spring if he needed to. He heard someone snicker.

Jamie glanced over at his parents, his face pale. Then he looked down at his dog. "Please, Barkley. You've got to pay attention," the boy pleaded.

Barkley kept his eyes glued to the announcer. He was convinced that noisy thing in the man's hand was what Jamie was afraid of.

"Barkley, heel," said Jamie as he started forward. Suddenly Barkley felt the collar tighten on his neck. Barkley fell forward and scrambled to catch up.

Now he heard giggles. Barkley turned to see what was so funny. The giggles turned to laughs. Barkley could tell Jamie was upset.

Jamie turned to the left, but Barkley was too busy staring at the announcer to notice. He wobbled around the corner and again he had to hurry to catch up.

They were on the opposite side from the announcer now, and Barkley decided maybe he'd better pay attention to Jamie. He threw his shoulders back and lifted his head. He stayed right with Jamie in the fast and slow walks and the two turns. He even sat perfectly at the end. The crowd clapped, and Jamie and Barkley were on their way out of the arena.

The collie was next, and he drew his share of laughs for doing almost everything wrong. Then one after another, Barkley's classmates went through their paces to occasional hoots and hollers. Everyone was finding out that doing things in front of a crowd is a lot different from practicing in class.

Sarge and Devon were the last pair to go. Sarge heeled, turned, and changed speed right on cue. But he kept his tail down almost between his legs and wore a disgusted look on his face.

When Sarge had finished, the announcer said, "Now for the sit-stay. Please bring your dogs into the arena and line up along the far side facing the judge. Space your dogs at least three feet apart. We don't want any new friendships started during this exercise."

Everyone laughed. The kids put their dogs into sitting positions while the announcer waited.

"Okay," he continued, "if your dog should move before this is over, he's disqualified. If that happens, return to your dog and hold him still until we're finished. Ready? Leave your dogs."

"Stay!" said the chorus of kids and hands waved in front of dogs' faces. The kids walked to the far side of the arena and turned around.

A cute mutt was right on his owner's heels, and the little girl started to cry. She grabbed her dog around the neck and held him close. The collie got up and wandered to the middle of the arena. Its owner rushed out to grab the dog. After a few more minutes, two other dogs got up and their masters rushed to grab them.

Barkley, however, remembered the squirt gun. He knew what he was supposed to do, and he wanted Jamie to be proud of him. He settled down for a long wait. He yawned and let his eyes wander over the crowd.

He saw ice cream cones, hot dogs, even cookies, and his mouth watered. A girl walked by with a cat in her arms, and he longed to chase it. He saw a little boy flipping something around on the end of a string. Barkley thought how much fun it would be to play tug of war with him. But he didn't move.

Suddenly, something caught Barkley's eye that he couldn't ignore. He looked over at

Jamie to see if he was coming yet, but his boy was still just standing there. Barkley knew Jamie wanted him to stay put, but the dog just couldn't.

In one huge bound, Barkley was over the rope around the arena and on his way.

## *Thirteen*

"**B**arkley, come back!" shouted Mrs. Boggs.

The dog heard people laughing and saw them pointing at him. He glanced over his shoulder to see that the sit-stay was over at last. He saw Jamie leap the fence and tear after him.

"Barkley, wait!" cried his boy. But Barkley couldn't wait. What he'd seen was much more important than any dog show.

Barkley reached a thick group of people. He tried to push his way through, but they wouldn't move. Desperately he tried to see around them. Had he only thought he'd seen her? he wondered.

Finally two people stepped aside, and Barkley saw several people sitting together talking quietly. He rushed forward and sat near them.

"Ruff, ruff," he said softly.

Two men turned to look at Barkley and shook their heads. Then the last person—the most important person—looked down at him from her wheelchair. For a second she didn't seem to know him either. Barkley licked her hand and said, "Ruff?"

The old woman's eyes suddenly brightened and she gasped. "Oh, my goodness," she said. "I can't believe it's you. But it must be."

She held her arms open wide. Barkley jumped right up on her lap and licked her face. He was so happy to see Mrs. Williams. She was all right!

"It's my little Love," she said, hugging him so hard it almost hurt. "I'm sure of it, but where did he come from?"

Barkley wagged his tail like crazy. He

wiggled all over with delight. It felt so good to have her petting him again.

"Mom, what's going on?" the man behind Mrs. Williams's chair asked. "Is that dog bothering you?"

"Never!" she replied with a big grin. "This is the dog I was telling you about, Tim. He's the one who brought help the day I fell."

Tim stared at Barkley. "That's him?" he asked. "Are you sure?"

"Yes, I'm almost certain it is," Mrs. Williams said, scratching Barkley behind the ears. "See how happy he is to see me?"

The two men looked at each other and shrugged. "Well, then," said Tim, "he deserves the royal treatment."

Just then Jamie came running up. When he saw Barkley in Mrs. Williams's lap, his face fell.

"Oh, gosh, I'm so sorry, ma'am," he said. "Barkley doesn't usually get so carried away. I mean, he's friendly and all, but he doesn't

usually jump right up in people's laps. Come here, Barkley."

Barkley didn't move. He couldn't leave Mrs. Williams yet, not after missing her so much.

"His name is Barkley?" asked Mrs. Williams. "Is he your dog?"

"Yes," Jamie said miserably. "We were in the dog show, and Barkley just took off. He was supposed to sit and stay, and he ruined everything. I guess he's not very smart."

"Not very smart?" she said with a giggle. "I'd say he was just about the smartest dog I've ever met."

Jamie looked at her strangely. "What do you mean? He just got himself disqualified from the dog show. We practiced and practiced, and I wanted to win."

The woman stroked Barkley's neck thoughtfully. "Yes, I can understand your disappointment," she said. "Especially when he seemed to be running away. But your dog and I are good friends. I think he's been worried about me."

Jamie looked puzzled. "I don't understand."

"Your dog visits me every day," she explained. "We have a great time. We play fetch, have lunch together, and check out my flowers. We even take naps together on my porch."

"No," said Jamie. "That can't be Barkley. He's locked in the garage every day while my parents work and I'm at school."

Jamie's parents came up then. "Yes, that's right," said Mrs. Boggs. "He's always there when Mom comes home, isn't he, Jamie?"

"Yeah, he's always under that old desk lying on his bed of rags. When I open the garage door, he always runs up to me. He's never gotten out."

The beginner handlers' part of the dog show was over, so some of the other kids wandered over. They nudged each other and whispered among themselves.

Mrs. Williams introduced herself and her sons. Then she said, "So you think I have the wrong dog, eh? Well, let's try a little test to see if he's really the one who visits me."

"A test?" said Mrs. Boggs. "What kind of a test?"

"You'll see," Mrs. Williams said mysteriously.

She set Barkley on the ground and reached inside her purse for a cookie. It was peanut butter, Barkley's favorite. "Cookie time," she said cheerfully.

Barkley wagged his tail with delight. He sat, tipped his head to one side so that one ear stood up, raised his right paw, and said, "Ruff."

Mrs. Williams grinned from ear to ear. "See?" she declared. "That's a little game we play. I guess you taught it to him, young man?"

"Well, yes. Yes, I did," Jamie mumbled. "But I just don't understand how he . . ."

Still smiling, Mrs. Williams interrupted. "Oh, your dog and I have shared a lot. In fact, you could say he saved my life."

Mr. Boggs moved in closer. "What? When?"

"Well, last week, I had a bad fall in my

122

kitchen," she began. "I cracked a bone in my leg as you can see by this cast. I also got knocked out when I fell."

She hesitated, then continued. "Somehow Barkley here knew I needed help. He went over to my neighbor's and barked and barked until she followed him. She got an ambulance."

"Barkley did all that?" Jamie asked in amazement. "But I had so much trouble just getting him to heel and stay."

"Yep," said Tim. "He sure did. Mom talks about him all the time. It's hard for me or my brother Darrel to check on Mom as often as we should. She needs a dog like Barkley to keep an eye on her. Well, what I'm trying to say is . . . we'd like to buy Barkley."

"Yes, just name your price," said Darrel. "Barkley's done so much for her already."

"No!" cried Jamie. "Barkley is my dog. He's not for sale."

"Jamie's right," said Mr. Boggs. "Barkley's a member of the family, and he's not for sale. But

I do have an idea. Mrs. Williams, how would you like to be Barkley's official daytime babysitter? We'd supply all his food, of course."

"And I'll supply plenty of cookies," Mrs. Williams added.

"Hey, I like cookies too," Jamie chimed in. "Maybe I could visit Mrs. Williams sometimes too. Maybe I could even cut her grass now and then."

Tim laughed. "Great idea," he said. "There's plenty of work to do, and we'd be happy to pay you for it."

"Then it's a deal," said Mrs. Boggs.

"Yes," said Mrs. Boggs. "But I still can't figure out how Barkley manages to get out of the garage every day. That mystery is driving me crazy."

"I'm sure you'll figure it out one of these days," said Mrs. Williams, beaming down at Barkley. "And I'm thrilled about Barkley and me babysitting each other. What do you think, Barkley?"

Of course, Barkley couldn't understand what the humans were saying. But he could tell all his favorite people were happy, and that made him happy too. "Ruff, ruff," he said.

Finally Barkley's family said good-bye to Mrs. Williams and her sons. They went back to the dog show arena just in time to see Melissa being handed a trophy.

"All right, Melissa!" Jamie yelled. "Way to go, Sadie!"

"What are you cheering about?" asked Devon, suddenly appearing at Jamie's side. "That mutt of yours didn't even finish the class."

Jamie turned and quickly put himself between Sarge and Barkley. Devon waved a red ribbon under Jamie's nose, but the shepherd merely looked bored.

Jamie's eyes flashed and his mouth came open, but then he stopped. "Congratulations on the ribbon," he said.

"Who cares about that?" said one of the

other kids. "Barkley's a real live hero."

"Yeah," agreed the girl with the collie. "He went to get help for an old lady who got knocked out. He saved her life, and that's more important than any old ribbon."

"No way!" said Devon. "Barkley's too stupid. You're just making that up because you're jealous of Sarge and me."

"No, they aren't," Mr. Boggs said quietly. "It's nice that you won a ribbon, Devon, but Barkley's smarter than you thought. He really did save Mrs. Williams's life."

"I think Barkley should get a ribbon, too," said Danielle.

Jamie shook his head. "Nah," he said. "We don't need a ribbon to prove Barkley's a great dog. I'm so proud of him I'm about to burst my buttons." He patted Barkley's head, and the dog wiggled with pleasure.

Just then a woman and a man with a camcorder rushed up. "Excuse me," the woman said. "We're from Channel 10 Action News, and we'd like to do a story about this dog and the woman he saved. Can you help us find her?"

Jamie and Barkley led the way to Mrs. Williams. Barkley sat next to her wheelchair, and Jamie stood beside her. The humans talked and the camera whirred. But Barkley was bored.

Mrs. Williams was watching him closely. "Are you hungry?" she said at last. "Do you want a cookie?"

Suddenly Barkley was all ears. He sat up straight, tilted his head to one side so that one ear stood up. Then he raised his right paw. "RUFF!" he said.

"Got it!" said the cameraman. "What a story!"

## About the Author

MARILYN D. ANDERSON grew up on a dairy farm in Minnesota. Her love for animals and her twenty-plus years of training and showing horses are reflected in many of her books.

A former music teacher, Marilyn taught band and choir for seventeen years. She specializes in percussion and violin. She stays busy training young horses, riding in dressage shows, working at a library, giving piano lessons, and, of course, writing books. Marilyn and her husband live in Bedford, Indiana.

*Nobody Wants Barkley* is the sequel to *Come Home, Barkley.*